Hushabye, Bearcub

Strawberrie Donnelly

Columbus, Ohio

Hushabye, Bearcub,
the end of the day.
Stars smile softly
as we wend our way.

Home at last, Bearcub,
safely indoors.
Mugs of hot chocolate
to warm our cold paws.

Peek-a-boo, Bearcub,
now where can you be?
Just five more minutes
and then B-E-D!

Ups-a-bye, Bearcub!
Come, sleepyhead.
Quietly, *quietly*,
upstairs to bed.

Splash-a-bye, Bearcub, paws, ears, and toes. Dry your wet whiskers, hop into clean clothes.

Brush-a-bye, Bearcub,
gently, that's it.
Now for the best part,
one, two, three . . . spit!

Into bed, Bearcub,
Teddy and all.
Tuck in the blankets
'round big cubs and small!

Story time, Bearcub,
snuggle down deep.
A much-loved old favorite,
to send you to sleep.

Hug-a-bye, Bearcub,
cuddle you tight.
Dozy and cozy
I kiss you goodnight.